The Barber Who Wanted to Pray
Copyright © 2011 text R. C. Sproul and illustrations T. Lively Fluharty
Published by Crossway
        1300 Crescent Street
        Wheaton, Illinois 60187

Cover Design: Josh Dennis
Cover illustration: T. Lively Fluharty
First printing 2011
Printed in China

Scripture quotations are from the ESV® Bible (*The Holy Bible, English Standard Version*®), copyright © 2001 by Crossway Bibles. Used by permission. All rights reserved.

Hardcover ISBN: 978-1-4335-2703-6
PDF ISBN: 978-1-4335-2704-3
Mobipocket ISBN: 978-1-4335-2705-0
ePub ISBN: 978-1-4335-2706-7

Library of Congress Cataloging-in-Publication Data

Sproul, R. C. (Robert Charles), 1939–2017
 The barber who wanted to pray / R. C. Sproul ; [illustrations T. Lively Fluharty].
   p. cm.
Summary: One night after family devotions, Delaney asks her father to teach her to do better at prayer and he relates the story of Master Peter, a sixteenth-century barber who made the same request of Martin Luther.
ISBN 978-1-4335-2703-6 (hc)
[1. Prayer—Fiction. 2. Christian life—Fiction. 3. Luther, Martin, 1483–1546—Fiction. 4. Barbers—Fiction. 5. Family life—Fiction.] I. Fluharty, T. Lively, ill. II. Title.

PZ7.S7693Bar 2011
 [Fic]—dc22
                                      2011003312

Crossway is a publishing ministry of Good News Publishers

The BARBER
WHO WANTED *to* PRAY

R. C. SPROUL

CROSSWAY

WHEATON, ILLINOIS

Every night at dinner, Mr. McFarland gathered his family together for devotions. Mr. and Mrs. McFarland had six children, two boys and four girls. The children's names were Donovan, Reilly, Maili, Erin Claire, Delaney, and Shannon.

It was Mr. McFarland's practice to read a portion of Scripture every night and give a short explanation of it. Then he would ask each of the children to recite memory verses from the Bible and to answer catechism questions. Finally, Mr. McFarland would lead the family in prayer. Each of the children would participate in the prayers in his or her own way.

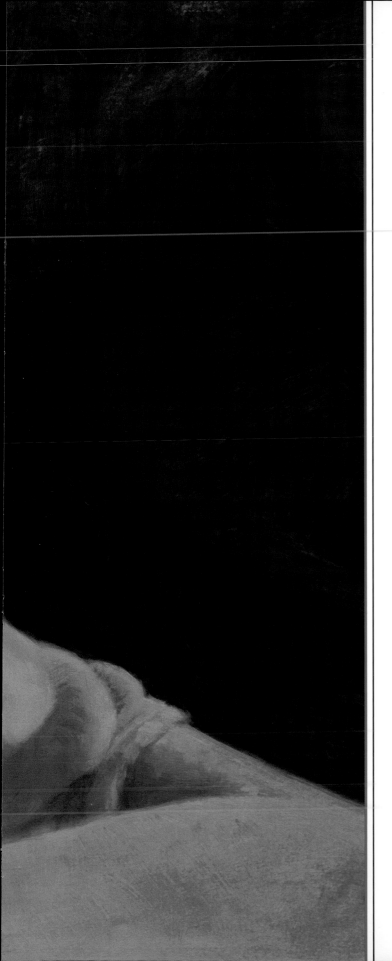

One night, just after devotions had ended with the singing of a favorite hymn, the McFarlands' daughter Delaney spoke up. "Daddy," she said, "your prayers are beautiful. Sometimes I want to cry for joy when I listen to your prayers. But *my* prayers seem so simple and weak. I'm almost embarrassed and ashamed to pray out loud. Daddy, can you teach me how to pray in a way that will make Jesus happy and will make me feel more comfortable?"

M r. McFarland smiled. "I understand how you feel, Delaney," he said. "When I was younger, I felt exactly the same way. I wasn't sure how to pray. About all I knew when I was your age was the table grace:

> God is great, God is good,
> and we thank Him for this food.

"Oh, yes, I also knew my nighttime prayer:

> Now I lay me down to sleep,
> I pray the Lord my soul to keep,
> If I should die before I wake
> I pray the Lord my soul to take.

"But other than those two simple prayers, about the only thing I could say in prayer was, 'Dear God, please bless Mommy and Daddy and my brother and sister and Uncle Joe and Aunt Sue.' Then my grandfather told me a story that changed everything for me. Do you think you might like to hear the story?"

Delaney said, "Yes, I surely would." The other children, who had been listening to the conversation between Delaney and their father, nodded eagerly, too. So Mr. McFarland told his children this story.

Once upon a time, in a village far across the sea, there lived a barber. Everyone in the town knew him. He not only cut men's hair and shaved their beards, but he could do all sorts of things that people needed to have done. The villagers called him simply "Master Peter."

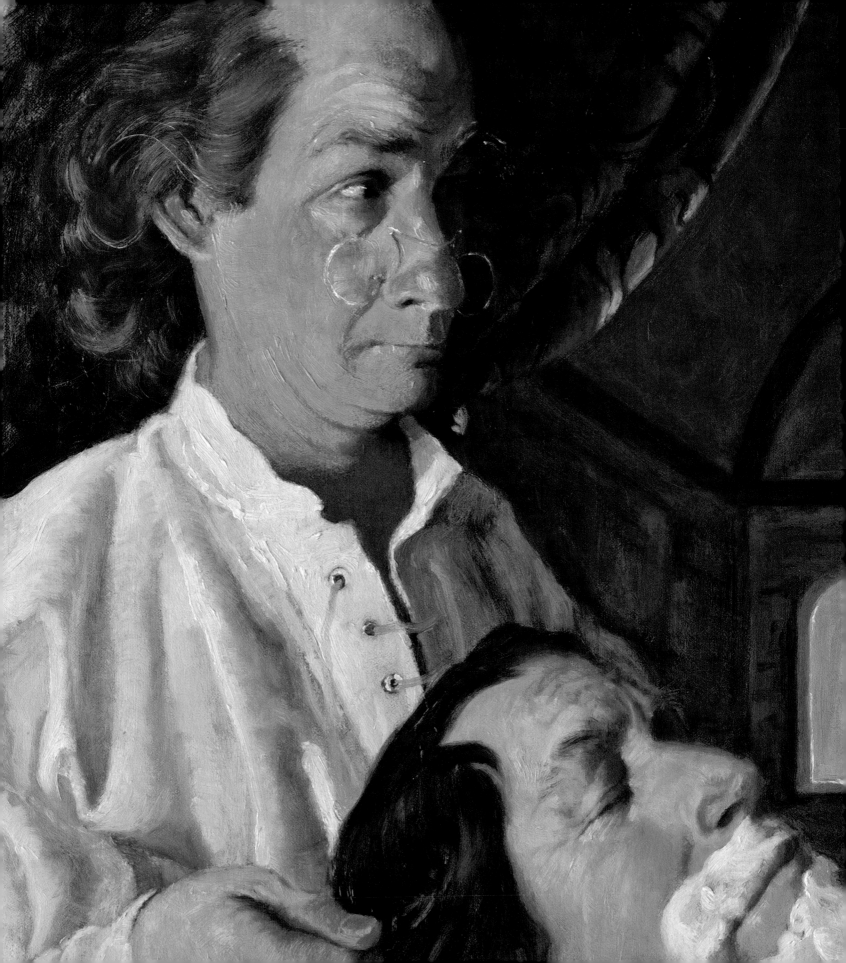

One morning, one of the village men came in for a shave. Master Peter put a cloth around the man's neck to keep the whiskers from falling down his shirt, lathered up the man's chin, got out his razor, and began to give the man a shave.

While the barber was shaving the man, the door opened and a new customer walked into his shop. Master Peter recognized the man immediately, for he was an outlaw. The emperor of the land had promised a large reward for anyone who could capture him—dead or alive. Master Peter knew the authorities would take this man away if they could get their hands on him.

When Master Peter finished shaving the first gentleman, he sent him on his way and motioned for the outlaw to have a seat.

Master Peter asked, "What can I do for you today, sir?"

The outlaw said, "I would like to have a haircut and a shave."

Master Peter began to snip away at the man's hair, trimming it neatly. He then rubbed soap lather on his face to prepare him for a shave. Peter took out his razor, and as he sharpened it on the strop beside the barber chair, his hands began to tremble as he thought about the importance of the man who was sitting in his chair. He calmed himself down and began to shave the man's face, moving down from his cheeks to his chin to his neck. Peter's razor was pressed very gently against the outlaw's neck. All Peter had to do was to press hard on the razor and he would cut the man's throat, killing him instantly. Then Peter could go to the emperor and say that he had taken care of the outlaw, and he could claim the reward, which would make him rich.

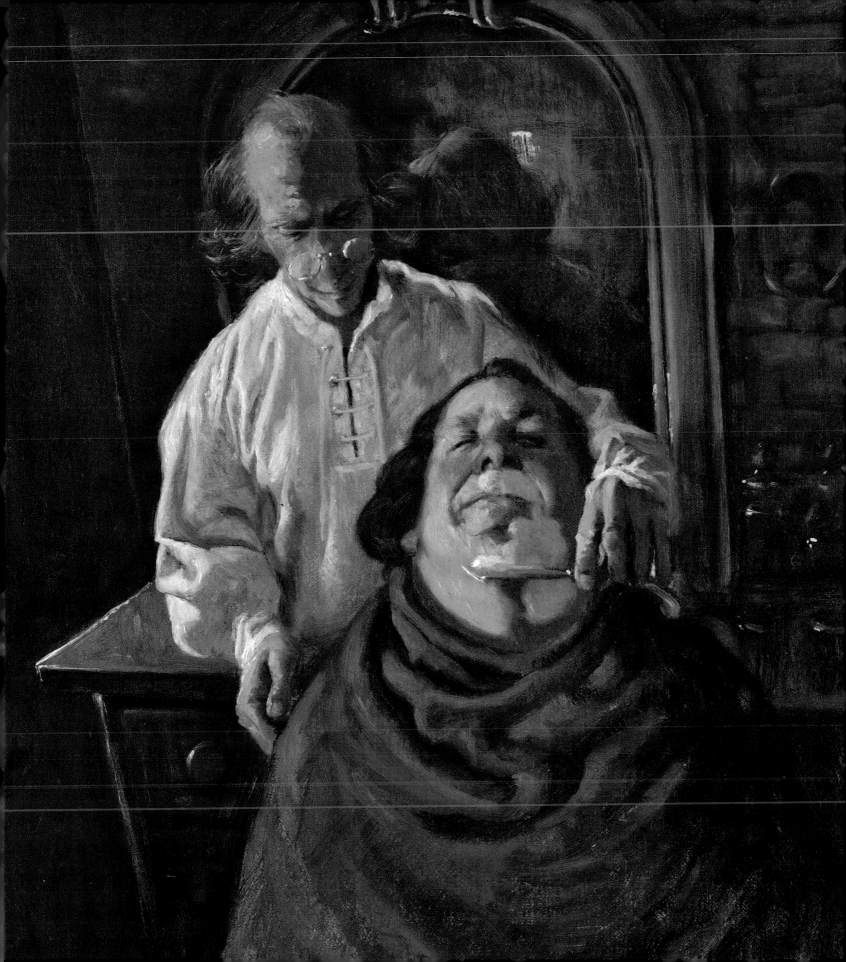

But as his razor touched the man's neck, Master Peter thought to himself, "There's not enough money in all the world to make me kill this man. He is my hero."

Master Peter knew the story of the man in his chair. The man had been a monk, then a knight, and now he was a world-famous professor at the university in Peter's town. The world had been changed and the whole church was better because the reformer had been brave enough to stand up for the truth of the gospel of Jesus, as no one had since the days of the apostles. No one had so much courage as he.

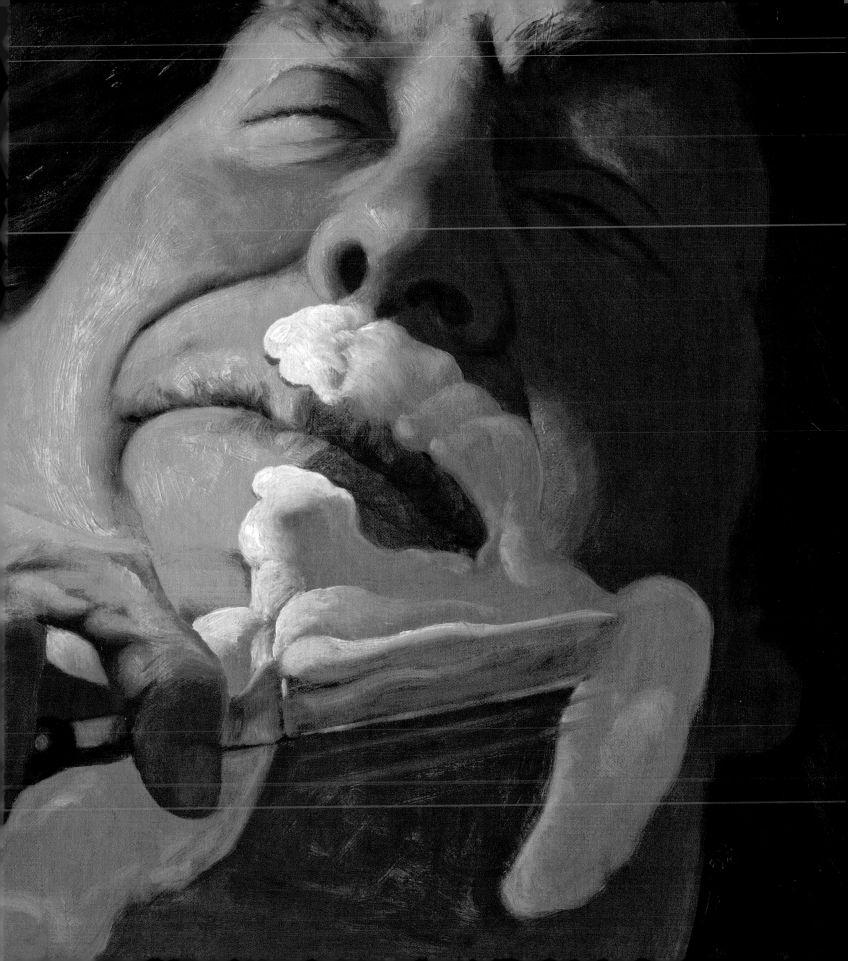

The name of the outlaw in the chair was *Martin Luther*, the man whose protest had started the Protestant Reformation and recovered the gospel from darkness. But because his teachings had disturbed some of the authorities, including the emperor himself, those who were opposed to him had convinced the emperor to banish Professor Luther. Now they wanted to capture him and burn him at the stake. But the people who had discovered the truth of the gospel of Jesus because of this man's teaching loved him so much that they would rather lay down their lives than see him captured and executed. Dr. Luther's barber, Master Peter, was one of those people. Peter would never betray his hero.

Suddenly, Peter had an idea. He had been struggling with his prayers, and Dr. Luther was famous for his prayer life. He decided to ask Dr. Luther for his advice while he was sitting in the barber chair.

Peter said, "Dr. Luther, I know who you are. It is a privilege for me to have you in my barbershop today. I wonder whether I may ask you a question."

Dr. Luther said, "Of course, you may. How can I help you?"

Peter said, "I have a problem. I try to pray every night, but sometimes I feel that my prayers never go any further than the ceiling. I know that you pray for hours every day. There's probably no one who knows how to pray better than you do. Dr. Luther, do you think you could help me learn to pray better?"

Dr. Luther said, "That's a wonderful question, my friend. My students ask me very deep questions all the time about God and the Bible and church life, but rarely do they ask me about how to grow as a Christian. Nothing makes me happier than to learn that you want to pray in a deeper way. Let me go back to my study and think about it, and perhaps I can write down a few ideas that will help you pray more effectively."

T hank you, Dr. Luther," Peter said. Then he quickly finished Dr. Luther's shave.

When Dr. Luther got back to his study, he picked up his pen and began to write instructions for Master Peter. Dr. Luther wrote more than fifty books during his lifetime, but perhaps the smallest and shortest book he ever wrote was the one he wrote especially for his barber, Master Peter. In this book, Dr. Luther explained his method for prayer. He called the little book *A Simple Way to Pray*.

When the book was finished, Dr. Luther went back to the barbershop and gave the first copy to Master Peter. Peter couldn't believe that the great Martin Luther had taken time to write a book just for him so that he could learn how to pray.

D r. Luther said, "To begin with, you must learn three things by memory. The first is the Lord's Prayer, the second is the Ten Commandments, and the third is the Apostles' Creed."

Then Dr. Luther went on to explain that once Peter knew these things by heart, he could use them to help himself pray. "For example," Dr. Luther said, "you begin by praying through the Lord's Prayer."

Peter asked, "Do you mean that all I have to do is just pray the Lord's Prayer every night?"

Our Father in heaven,
Hallowed be Your name.
Your kingdom come.
Your will be done
On earth as it is in heaven.
Give us this day our daily bread.
And forgive us our debts,
As we forgive our debtors.
And do not lead us into temptation,
But deliver us from the evil one.
For Yours is the kingdom
and the power and the glory forever.
Amen.

N o," Dr. Luther said, "that's not what I mean. It's a wonderful thing to do, but what I mean by praying *through* the Lord's Prayer is doing something like this: Think about the first petition in the Lord's Prayer, 'Our Father in heaven, hallowed be your name.' When you think about these words, allow your mind and your heart to give careful attention to what these words say, and let them move you to deeper prayer. Say the first line of the prayer and then begin to pray like this:

O God, it's hard for me to believe that You are really willing to be my heavenly Father. In our family, we have our father, whom we love, but You are the Father of all of us who put our faith in Jesus. It's because Jesus is Your Son and through Him You have adopted us into Your family, that we have the privilege to pray to You as our Father. We know that You don't have an address here in our village, but You reside in heaven itself. You're not our earthly father, You're our heavenly Father; and You are the one who owns the whole world. It is wonderful that we have a Father who owns everything to whom I can come in my prayers.

Jesus taught us to say 'hallowed be your name.'

Father help me to understand that there's nothing more important in my life and in my prayer than to give reverence and worship to Your name. Lord, guard my tongue, that I may never use Your name in a foolish or corrupt manner, but that when I speak of You and when I think of You, my heart will be moved to respect and adore You."

Dr. Luther said to Peter, "Do you understand what I mean by praying *through* the Lord's Prayer? You can pray through these parts of the Lord's Prayer every day and never make the same prayer twice. You can think about one portion of it and give your attention to that, and your prayers will rise in excitement and in joy."

Then Dr. Luther said, "Now think about praying through the Ten Commandments. The first commandment says, 'You shall have no other gods before me.' You can pray something like this:

Lord God, we know that the world is filled with people who worship idols and statues, who believe in many gods, and yet You and You alone are God. Sometimes there are things in my life that I put ahead of You, things that become my idols. Forgive me when I do that. Help me not to allow myself to have any other gods in Your sight."

Master Peter was very excited. "I see what you mean," he said.

Dr. Luther grinned. "You can go through each one of the Ten Commandments in that manner," he said, "or you can turn your attention to the Apostles' Creed. It begins with, 'I believe in God, the Father Almighty'; as you begin to think about that, you begin to think of the power God has, the strength that He displays. Our children think that we, as their earthly fathers, are so strong that we can do anything. But we are complete weaklings compared to God, because He is almighty, and we love Him not just for what He can do for us but for Who He is.

"So we can pray and pray and never get tired of praying. We can never run out of things to pray about if we focus our attention on the Lord's Prayer, on the Ten Commandments, and on the Apostles' Creed."

Master Peter could not thank Dr. Luther enough for teaching him the secret to a simple way to pray.

When Mr. McFarland ended his story, he said to his children, "Do you see why every night during our devotions I want to make sure that you are learning the Lord's Prayer, the Ten Commandments, and the Apostles' Creed? From now on at our devotions, when you pray, I'm going to ask you to practice praying in the simple way that Dr. Luther taught his barber."

Delaney said, "Thank you for telling us that story, Daddy. I can hardly wait to try Dr. Luther's way to pray. In fact, can we have family devotions again tonight so we can try it?"

The other children said, "Oh, yes, Daddy, please!"

Mr. McFarland was delighted to see his children's new interest in prayer. He said with a smile, "Let's pray."

THE TEN COMMANDMENTS

1. You shall have no other gods before me.

2. You shall not make for yourself a carved image, or any likeness of anything that is in heaven above, or that is in the earth beneath, or that is in the water under the earth. You shall not bow down to them or serve them, for I the LORD your God am a jealous God, visiting the iniquity of the fathers on the children to the third and the fourth generation of those who hate me, but showing steadfast love to thousands of those who love me and keep my commandments.

3. You shall not take the name of the LORD your God in vain, for the LORD will not hold him guiltless who takes his name in vain.

4. Remember the Sabbath day, to keep it holy. Six days you shall labor, and do all your work, but the seventh day is a Sabbath to the LORD your God. On it you shall not do any work, you, or your son, or your daughter, your male servant, or your female servant, or your livestock, or the sojourner who is within your gates. For in six days the LORD made heaven and earth, the sea, and all that is in them, and rested on the seventh day. Therefore the LORD blessed the Sabbath day and made it holy.

5. Honor your father and your mother, that your days may be long in the land that the LORD your God is giving you.

6. You shall not murder.

7. You shall not commit adultery.

8. You shall not steal.

9. You shall not bear false witness against your neighbor.

10. You shall not covet your neighbor's house; you shall not covet your neighbor's wife, or his male servant, or his female servant, or his ox, or his donkey, or anything that is your neighbor's. (Exodus 20:3–17)

THE LORD'S PRAYER

Pray then like this: "Our Father in heaven, hallowed be your name. Your kingdom come, your will be done, on earth as it is in heaven. Give us this day our daily bread, and forgive us our debts, as we also have forgiven our debtors. And lead us not into temptation, but deliver us from evil." (Matthew 6:9–13)

THE APOSTLES' CREED

I believe in God, the Father Almighty,
Maker of heaven and earth.

And in Jesus Christ, His only Son, our Lord;
Who was conceived by the Holy Ghost,
born of the virgin Mary,
suffered under Pontius Pilate,
was crucified, dead, and buried.
He descended into hell.
The third day He arose again from the dead.
He ascended into heaven,
and sitteth on the right hand of God the Father Almighty;
from thence he shall come to judge the quick and the dead.

I believe in the Holy Ghost;
the holy catholic church;
the communion of saints;
the forgiveness of sins;
the resurrection of the body;
and the life everlasting.

Amen.